Little Flo did not do ANY of these things.

She liked to eat naughty treats ...

chase frogs
through mucky puddles ...

One day, Daddy Duck and Flo were off to visit Auntie Jenna's new nest. Daddy Duck puffed up his feathery chest and said, in his most serious deep duckie voice:

"Now then, Flo. You have to FOLLOW ME all the way. No chasing or hiding, or you'll get lost."

"Yes, Daddy, I promise,"
said Little Flo.

So off they went.

"Why don't we sing a song
as you follow along?" said Daddy.
"I LOVE singing, Daddy," said Flo.
"I can sing VERY high
and VERY LOUD."

"OK, Flo, but listen to me first...

We're off to somewhere new.
So stick to me like glue...

FOLLOW ME, FLO!

Come on, let's go!
We're sure to be
there soon.

Follow me UP...

Follow me DOWN...

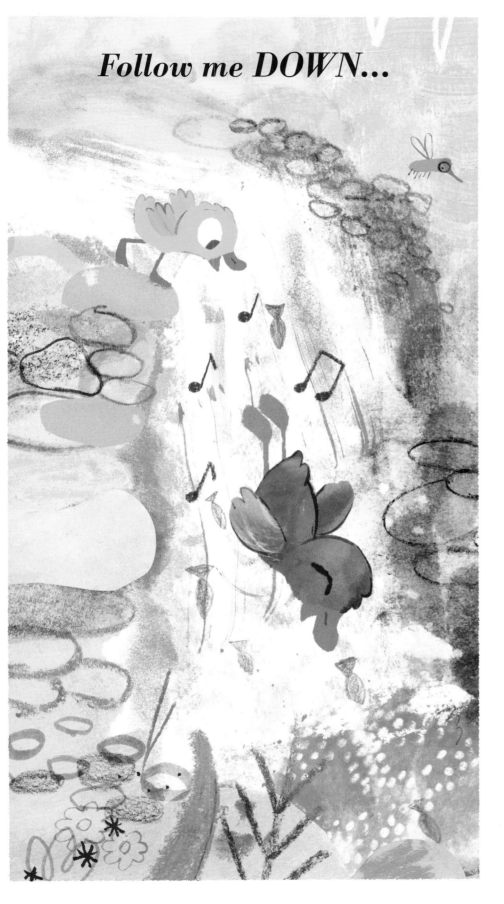

Look straight ahead, and NOT AROUND!

Follow me IN...

Follow me OUT...

If you fall behind,
just give me a
SHOUT!
Yes, follow me,
follow me, Flo..."

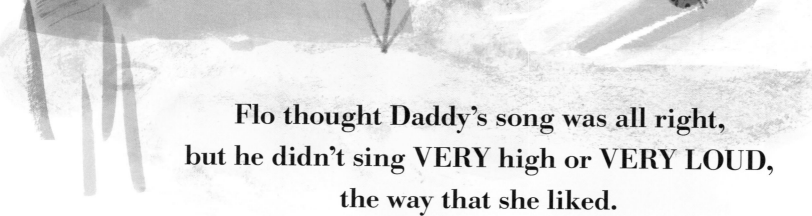

Flo thought Daddy's song was all right,
but he didn't sing VERY high or VERY LOUD,
the way that she liked.

So Flo made up her OWN song...

"*Follow, follow, follow me,*
I'm little duckie
FLO!

Follow, follow, follow me,

I'M SUPER-FAST, NOT SLOW.

UNDER...

OVER...

FUNFAIR

Now, Flo was SO carried away
singing her new song,
she didn't notice that she
WAS being followed –
and Roxy Fox definitely didn't
want a sing-along!

But Flo had lost sight of Dad
a long time ago.

Then, suddenly, she remembered ...
Daddy's song!
Quickly, she sang:

"Follow me UP...

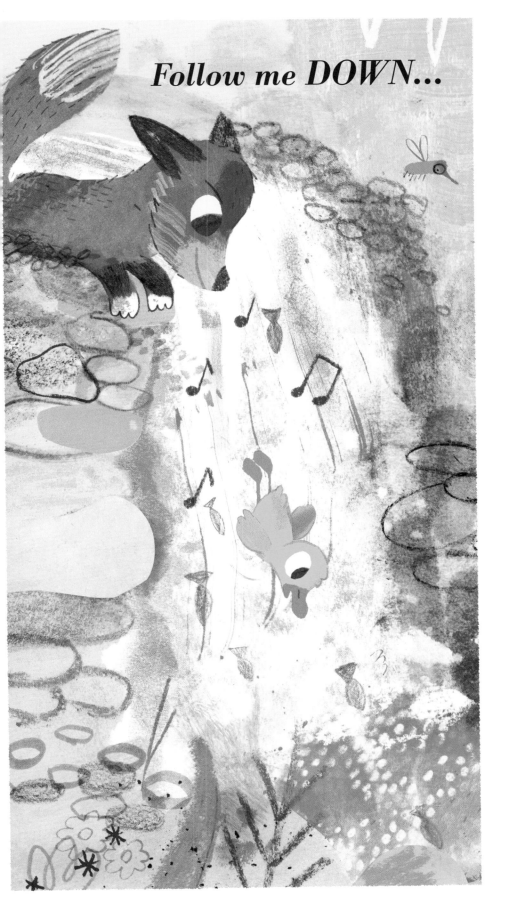

Follow me DOWN...

**Look straight ahead,
and
NOT
AROUND!**

Follow me
IN...

Follow me
OUT...

"Keep up, Flo! Very good following.
We're almost there," said Daddy Duck.

"I LOVE your Follow Song, Daddy," said Flo.
"It's my absolute favourite in the whole world."

And when they got to Auntie Jenna's new home,

oh, what a happy,
dizzy, duckie dance
they all had!

That night, Flo ate all of her seeds and berries
(like a good little duckie),

preened herself squeaky-clean (for the very first time),

and fell fast asleep (perfectly in a row).

And the next morning,
for being SO good at following on the way over,
Daddy Duck let Flo lead the way home...

*"Follow, follow, follow me,
I'm little duckie
FLO!"*